Aesop's Fables
The Lion and the Mouse

There was once a great lion who lived on the grassy plains, close to the edge of the jungle. Each day he roamed the grasslands, checking that all was well in his kingdom.

He feared no one,
but everyone
feared him.

The zebra mothers warned their children about the lion.

"Stay away from the lion.
Keep your distance
and all will be well."

And the elephant mothers warned their children too. "I am far too big for the lion to hunt, but you are small. **Stay close to me** and all will be well."

Now when it grew **too hot** during the day, the lion would walk into the jungle, where the shade of the trees meant it was cool and dark.

He would roam through the shady jungle until he reached his cave.

Here he slept for a few hours each day.

A family of mice also lived in the jungle. They had a nest in a hole in a tree, and each day the young mice were sent to look for food.

One of the little mice was **particularly curious**, and he often ventured further than his brothers and sisters.

One day, the mouse reached the edge of the jungle. He saw the great plains of grass and herds of animals.

He gasped in fear at the sight of the mighty lion on his rock, and scurried back into the jungle.

Each day, the little mouse saw the lion walking to his cave to sleep, and his curiosity got the better of him.

He just had to look inside the cave.

So one day, the mouse decided to visit the lion's cave. He knew the lion was on the plains, so he crept through the jungle until he arrived at the mouth of the cave.

Dare he go any further?

"ROAAAAR!"

A giant paw trapped the mouse. It was the lion! "Please let me go!" begged the mouse. "I wasn't causing trouble!"

"Well you ARE in trouble!" growled the lion. "What are you doing in my cave?"

"Just being curious, Sir, but if you let me go, I promise one day to do you a good turn."

The lion laughed. "As if you could help me, king of the beasts! But you are so small, and I suppose quite brave. Be gone – and NEVER come back here again!"

The mouse scampered away.

Some weeks later,
as he prowled through the
jungle, the lion walked into
a trap. A strong net of
ropes fell on top of him.

But the more he struggled to free himself, the more entangled he became. He realized the hunter would return soon.

Exhausted, he lay still and roared softly.

Then the lion saw a tiny creature standing in front of him. It was the mouse.

"Let me help you," squeaked the mouse, and he set to work gnawing the rope.

Before long, the ropes fell away from the lion and he gave a mighty shake. The mouse found himself **scooped up in a giant paw.**

"Thank you," growled the lion.

Suddenly the lion placed the mouse on his back. "Hold on tight to my mane," he instructed.

And then they were racing through the jungle. The mouse held on tightly, his eyes squeezed shut.